MY
FRIEND
BEAR

To friendship

ISBN 0-590-63830-0

12 11 10 9   0 1 2 3/0

Printed in the U.S.A.   14

First Scholastic printing, October 1998

This book has been typeset in Garamond.

MY FRIEND BEAR

Jez Alborough

SCHOLASTIC INC.
New York Toronto London Auckland Sydney

Eddie's walking with his teddy.
Eddie's teddy's name is Freddie.
"Oh, Freddie," said Eddie,
with a great big sigh.
"I feel sad, but I don't know why."
Freddie said nothing.
Eddie sighed again.
"I wish you could talk," he said.
And then . . .

"Wow! Look at that! Up there on that stone.
A giant teddy, all on his own.
We've seen him before, he belongs to the bear
who lives around these woods somewhere."

Suddenly something made Eddie turn around:
a snuffling, scuffling, bear sort of sound.
A great big voice whined, "Where's my teddy?"
"He's coming, he's coming, let's hide!" cried Eddie.

The great big bear came shuffling by,
then stopped with a sniff and started to cry.
"Oh, teddy," he whimpered, "what can I do?
I've got no friends, apart from you.
And you can't talk, and you don't care.
I'm such a sad and lonely bear."
Then, just as he brushed a tear from his eye . . .

a little voice whispered, "Please don't cry!
I'm all on my own, just like you,
with no one to talk to and nothing to do.
I'm a little bit lonely, too, you see.
If you want, you can talk to me."
The bear couldn't believe his ears.
He gulped and sniffed and wiped his tears.
"You can talk after all!" he cried.

"Of course I can talk," the voice replied.
The bear came closer
and scratched his head.
"Why didn't you talk before?" he said.
"Because I'm scared," said the voice,
"and small and shy,
and you're a great big bear,
that's why."

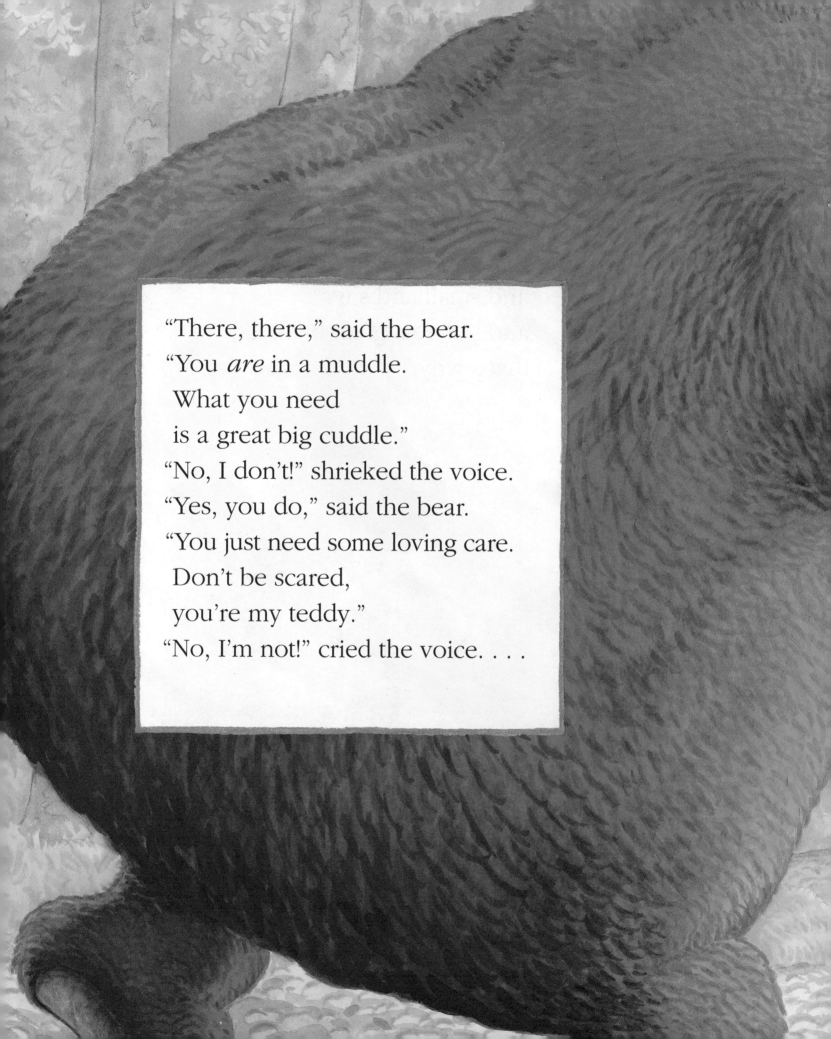

"There, there," said the bear.
"You *are* in a muddle.
What you need
is a great big cuddle."
"No, I don't!" shrieked the voice.
"Yes, you do," said the bear.
"You just need some loving care.
Don't be scared,
you're my teddy."
"No, I'm not!" cried the voice. . . .

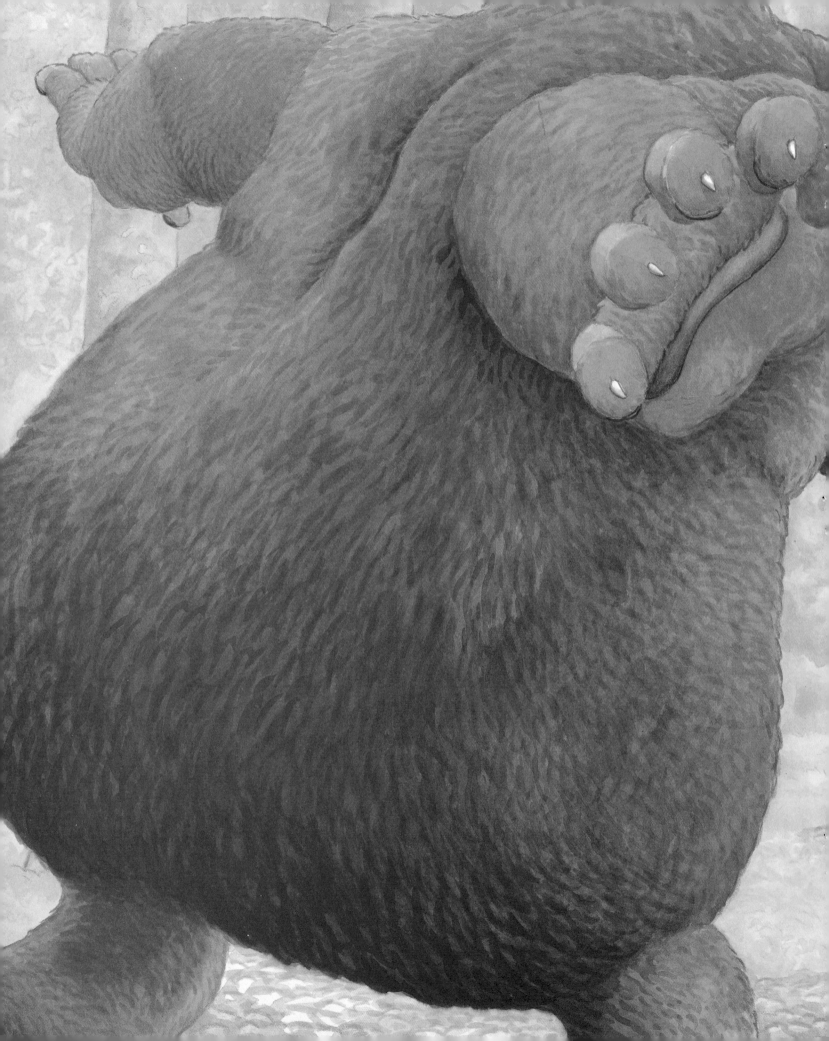

"It's me . . .
Eddie!"

The bear stared at Eddie
and clung to his teddy.
Eddie stared back
and hung on to Freddie.

Suddenly Eddie started to grin.

He felt a chuckle rise up from within.

He tried to stop it, but it wouldn't stay down.

"What's so funny?" asked the bear, with a frown.

"It's you," giggled Eddie.

"It's you, standing there.

You're such a great big silly bear!"

"No, I'm not," said the bear.

"Yes, you are!" yelped Eddie.

"You thought you had a talking teddy."

Then the bear began to snigger.
The smile on his face grew bigger and bigger.
His great big belly wiggled and jiggled.
"I am a silly bear," he giggled.
"A talking teddy—I thought it was true—
but all along it was really you."

The bear held out his giant-sized teddy,
crouched down behind it,
and said, "Hello, Eddie.
I'm a talking teddy—listen to me!
Aren't I clever? I'm only three."
Then Eddie wanted to have a go.
    He held up his teddy
        and squeaked, "Hello!
        My name's Freddie.
            How do you do?
            I can talk, and
            I'm only two!"

They laughed and they laughed
till their tummies were sore,
then they looked at each other
and laughed some more.
The bear started dancing and singing a song,
and he made up the words as he wobbled along.
"I'm silly," he sang, "and I don't care.
I'm such a great big silly bear!"
"Whahoo!" sang Eddie. "I'm as silly as you!
And your teddy and Freddie are silly, too."
All afternoon they played in the sun,
seeing just who was the silliest one.

When the sun began
to set in the sky,
they knew it was time
to say good-bye.

"We're friends," said Eddie.
The bear said, "Who?"
"You know," said Eddie,
"me and you."

The bear lifted Eddie
up for a hug,
hairy and beary,
safe and snug.

"Take care," he said.
"Look after Freddie!"
"We'll come back soon,"
whispered Eddie.

Then off they walked,
with a smile and a wave.
Back to a house,
and back to a cave.
Do you think that they're lonely?
Not anymore. . . .

That's what
having friends
is for.